For Mom

Copyright © 2004 by Tor Freeman

First U.S. edition 2004

Library of Congress Cataloging-in-Publication Data is available.

Library of Congress Catalog Card Number 2003060460

ISBN 0-7636-2452-7

2 4 6 8 10 9 7 5 3 1

Printed in Singapore

This book was typeset in Aunt Mildred.
The illustrations were done in gouache and pencil.

Candlewick Press
2067 Massachusetts Avenue
Cambridge, Massachusetts 02140

visit us at www.candlewick.com

HOORAY, I'M FIVE TODAY!

Tor Freeman

Hi, Tyler!

CANDLEWICK PRESS
CAMBRIDGE, MASSACHUSETTS

On Dinah's
fifth birthday,
Tyler planned a wonderful
surprise for her.
In the afternoon,
while they were painting
a picture together,
there was a knock at the door.
"I'll get it," said Tyler.

TOOT TOOT TOOT TOOT

Brown Rabbit
burst into the room,
playing a brass horn.
And what was
the tune?

"Happy Birthday
to You!"

Next Lemur came in with some flowers.
"Happy birthday, Dinah," she said.
"I'm five," said Dinah.

Then Croccy
popped in
and gave Dinah
an enormous
crocodile
hug.

SQUEEZE

"Hello, Croccy," said Dinah.

"It's my birthday."

"Happy birthday,"

said Croccy.

Blow harder!

And Croccy gave them all

one of her famous crocodile rides.

WHEEEEE!

The last to arrive, in a rush,
was Otter, with Dan and Jed Frog.
"Hop!" and "Pop!"
said Dan and Jed.
"Happy birthday, Dinah!"
said Otter.

He gave her
the red balloon.

For party games
they jumped rope
and played ring-around-the-rosy.

And they danced rock 'n' roll
while Otter blew the horn.

Then Tyler said, "It's time for cake.
But first, Dinah, shut your eyes."
This was going to be the best part:
Dinah's wonderful surprise.

1 ...

2 ...

3 ...

4 ...

5 ...

Wow!

What

an enormous

cake!

"Surprise!" shouted everyone, suddenly jumping out from behind the cake.

"HAPPY BIRTHDAY TO YOU!"